There once was a little girl named Macie who loved to look at the moon.

Every night when the stars began to twinkle, she would ask her mother and father, "Can we go look at the moon?" And holding hands, out they would go.

Each night the moon had a different look.

Some nights it was a curved sliver of light called a crescent moon.

Other nights it was dark and light and was called a half moon.

A cloud covering the moon made it a misty moon.

And if it looked dark and was difficult to see, that was a new moon.

But Macie's favorite moon was a full moon.
It looked like the biggest yellow ball she had ever seen!

One night Macie and her mother and father sat for a long time watching a full moon rise higher and higher in the sky.

Then her mother said,
"God made that moon just for you."
And Macie smiled.

After a time a baby sister named Megan was born.
Then another sister, Addie, was born. When they were older,
they would ask Macie, "Can we go look at the moon tonight?"
And holding hands, out they would go.

Some nights they saw a crescent moon.

Other nights they saw a half moon.

Sometimes they saw a misty moon.

And other times they saw a new moon.

But their favorite moon was a full moon.
It looked like the biggest yellow ball they had ever seen!

One night Macie, Megan, and Addie sat for a long time watching a full moon rise higher and higher in the sky.

Then Macie said to her sisters,
"God made that moon just for you." And they smiled.

If you go outside tonight, you may see

a crescent moon

a half moon

a misty moon

or a new moon.

But if you see a big, yellow FULL moon, remember
God made it just for you. And you will smile, too!

Macie and her family, 2013

Made in the USA
San Bernardino, CA
06 September 2016

MACIE's MOON

*"There once was a little girl named Macie
who loved to look at the moon.
Every night when the stars began to twinkle, she would
ask her mother and father, 'Can we go look at the moon?'
And holding hands, out they would go."*

Macie's Moon is a delightful story of a girl named Macie,
her family, and the beautiful phases of the moon!

Author **Joanna Dodd Lipscomb** lives in Texas and enjoys writing stories
about her grandchildren.

Eric Walls is an illustrator, animator, and designer. He illustrates children's
books through ericwallsillustration.com.

ISBN 9781503045767

90000

9 781503 045767